Surrender

Susan Coyle

authorHOUSE®

AuthorHouse™
1663 Liberty Drive
Bloomington, IN 47403
www.authorhouse.com
Phone: 1-800-839-8640

First published by AuthorHouse 4/7/2009

ISBN: 978-1-4389-5682-4 (sc)

Printed in the United States of America
Bloomington, Indiana

This book is printed on acid-free paper.

To all of you who have encouraged me to write this book and given me gems and tidbits along the way. Your involvement has enriched the story and I thank you, truly.

With special thanks to my family…

As a rose surrenders to nature

  A magnificent and fragrant blossom emerges.

As a surfer surrenders to the wave

  The force and direction of the water is his guide.

As I surrender to God

  I trust His Way will produce blessings to shine forth from within.

Susan Coyle

Chapter One

It was a little cool even though the sun was shining on this beautiful April morning. Meryl and Gary agreed it was a perfect day for gardening. There was nothing on the Nelson calendar, so they decided to seize the opportunity to do some spring cleaning outside. Charlie's plans, however, did not include gardening. This eleven-year-old wanted to go to the mall, see the new movie that just came out, maybe watch some television, play some videogames and lounge around in his pajamas - not necessarily in that order. So, at the Nelson's breakfast table on this early spring morning, there was a little disagreement between Charlie and his parents.

"What do you mean, you want me to work outside?" Charlie questioned, not believing his ears. "Are you kidding me? Why today, Dad? Kids are supposed to do nothing on Saturdays! I really don't want to help. It's not my garden; it's your garden anyway."

"We could use your help. Besides, we have nothing planned. We don't have to be at a baseball game or baseball practice or run any errands. We can spend time together as a family and get the yard spruced up. Come on, it won't be so bad, I promise," Dad tried to sound convincing.

"*You* may have nothing planned, but *I* have everything planned! I want to relax around the house, watch some TV or play the new videogame I got last week."

"Well, Charlie, *your* plans will have to wait." It was Mom's turn to chime in. "We need your help for an hour or so. The garden may be ours, but the backyard is most certainly yours. You play with your friends back there, and you are now old enough to help out around the house."

As Meryl and Gary got up from the table, Charlie's mom continued, "When you finish, put your dishes in the dishwasher, change in to your work clothes and meet us in the back. Don't be long." They both went outside to get started. Gary took in a deep breath of the fresh air, as he turned his face to the sun to feel its warmth. He heard the sounds of a lawnmower in the distance and chirping birds from above. He noticed the budding of the trees spotted with new growth.

They left Charlie sitting alone at the kitchen table with his thoughts. The aroma of fresh brewed coffee filled the air, and remnants of milk, cereal and sugar speckled the table.

Charlie was not happy and let everyone know it. He angrily raked the dead leaves from the flower beds, moaned as he pushed the wheelbarrow around while gathering fallen twigs, and placed the patio furniture from storage with a clatter.

"What's the matter with him?" Mr. Vento asked, as he and Gary watched Charlie.

"Oh, he's just sore because he has to help us clean up and he'd rather be inside playing videogames," Gary explained.

Mr. Vento has lived next door to the Nelson's for over ten years. Before becoming their neighbor, he and his wife lived in a larger house an hour or so away. Mr. Vento's wife died many years ago and throughout the years Mr. Vento realized he preferred a change of scenery and a smaller house. Through friends of his, he heard of this situation, where the owner of the house was looking for someone to live rent free in exchange for the upkeep of the property. Since Mr. Vento considered himself pretty handy around the house, he decided to inquire. He fell in love with the house and the neighborhood, and within three months he moved in. Now, more than ten years later, he has never regretted the decision, especially since he has such a nice relationship with the Nelson family. Gary and Meryl enjoy spending time with him while sharing a meal or when they could use another pair of hands. Charlie helps Mr. Vento with small house projects, building a new stage or creating an original story featuring new puppets. Dominic Vento is a puppeteer, and he enjoys sharing his craft with Charlie.

Mr. Vento and Gary watched Charlie as they chatted in the driveway. Mr. Vento had plans to work on the garage door. It was getting stuck in the same place every time it went up and down.

"So what are your plans tomorrow, Dominic?" Gary asked Mr. Vento.

"Nothing much," he replied as he was beginning to inspect the garage door.

"Meryl and I were wondering if you wanted to join us for Sunday dinner, around five?" Gary hoped he would say yes. Mr. Vento was like a father to him, and since it had been a few weeks since they'd seen him, Gary and Meryl wondered how he was doing.

"That sounds good. How about if I bring over a batch of my famous brownies? I know how much Charlie likes them." Mr. Vento always enjoyed himself at the Nelson's. Since his family lived so far away, it was a comfort for him to have neighbors who felt like family.

"Hey Dad, how about some help here. This was your idea to be out here working," Charlie yelled across the backyard, struggling to pull up a dead bush.

Looking at Dominic, Gary said, "We'll see you tomorrow night."

Then toward Charlie's direction he yelled, "I'm coming!"

Gary smiled at his wife and said, "Dominic will be here for dinner tomorrow night around five."

"Hey, not *that* bush Charlie, the one next to it. *That* one is actually a good one. The one next to it is the dead one," Charlie's dad instructed.

Chapter Two

"Good morning, Sport. Time to get up and get ready for school," Charlie's dad said as he entered Charlie's room and parted the curtains. "We're all running late, so let's get a move on."

Charlie noticed his father was dressed for work, which meant Charlie himself had overslept. "All right, all right. I'm getting up," Charlie said as he rolled over and put the pillow over his head.

"Come on, Charlie, I'm not fooling around. I'll meet you downstairs for breakfast." Charlie heard his dad's footsteps disappear down the stairs.

Gary could smell the fresh brewed coffee as he entered the kitchen. "Is Charlie up yet, Gary?" Meryl asked as she set out three bowls for cereal.

"He's working on it," he said as he leaned over and gave his wife a kiss good morning. Meryl looked at her husband and remarked, "You feeling okay? You don't look right. You're looking a bit pale." She put her hand on his head to check for a fever.

"Well, it was a pretty late night last night. It was such a nice dinner with Dominic. I miss spending time with him. We'll have to invite him over again real soon," Charlie's dad said as Charlie entered the kitchen.

"Next time we invite him over we're not playing cards. He won almost every hand. That was unbelievable! He got the perfect cards every time." Charlie spoke with frustration.

"He was having so much fun beating us. If there is any person I wouldn't mind losing to, it's Mr. Vento," Charlie's mom said as the three sat at the breakfast table.

Charlie was the first to finish. His father reminded him to hurry since Charlie needed to be at school early to study with his teacher for the math test tomorrow.

"I'm going, I'm going," Charlie muttered as he climbed the staircase.

"So what's on your schedule today?" Gary asked as he looked across the table.

"There is a PTA meeting this morning. Then I'm planning on meeting Sherry for lunch today. We always have such fun together. And have you seen the mounds of laundry in the hamper? Every Monday, this house needs to be tidied up after the weekend with the two of you!" Meryl answered. "And that's my day! How about you? What does the art teacher at Lincoln Elementary have planned for today?"

"This week we're starting a new unit on pottery. I have a different project for each grade, from the kindergarteners who will make monster sculptures to the fifth graders who will make a plate of food. Some kids were telling me they plan on making spaghetti and meatballs or a taco plate! I think it will all look great when it is time for the art show."

Meryl could see and hear the enthusiasm in her husband's voice as he explained his plans. She knew how much teaching meant to him. He was very fortunate to be doing a job he loved.

Charlie came dashing down the stairs, moving at the "I'm really late for school" speed. His dad was already waiting for him in the car. One benefit of having his dad teach at his school was that Charlie didn't have to walk to school every morning. As Meryl waved from the kitchen door, she turned around and realized her day began with cleaning the kitchen. There were still dirty dishes from last night's dinner with Mr. Vento, and Mr. Vento's empty brownie plate she'd have to return. Once piled high with a tower of delicious brownies, now empty!

"Okay, Meryl, just get started somewhere and keep moving forward till you're done," she said to herself as she opened the dishwasher and began to load dirty dishes.

Chapter Three

"Hey Mom, I'm home!" Charlie hollered as he came through the front door. That's Charlie's daily routine: leave for school from the kitchen door which is closest to the car and return from school through the front door because his mom made an area for him to throw down his backpack and coat. He could hear walking around upstairs but didn't get a response so he hollered a little bit louder this time, "Hey Mom, I'm home!"

He listened and heard the muffled words, "Hey Charlie, be down in a minute," which came from a bedroom where Meryl was putting away laundry. As she was heading down the stairs, Meryl could hear Charlie opening the oven to see what was baking.

She startled him when she entered the kitchen and said, "Since we ate up all of Mr. Vento's brownies last night, I decided to bake sugar cookies today. Another one of your favorites!"

He quickly turned around and closed the oven. "Hi, Mom."

"Hi, Charlie," and she gave him a kiss on the cheek. "How was your day?" she asked.

"It was okay," he said. That's what he said every day!

"Learn anything new today?" she wondered.

"No, nothing really," again, his usual response. "I'm hoping Dad will want to play catch with me in the backyard when he gets home. I'd like to get my arm ready for baseball."

"Dad was talking about wanting to coach your baseball team again this year since he had such a good time last year. I'm sure he'll want to catch with you. He has to get in shape, too," she admitted as she took the cookies out of the oven. She put a few on a plate and handed it to Charlie, along with a glass of milk, as he thanked her with a kiss on the cheek. He disappeared to the TV room.

Not long after Charlie arrived home, Meryl heard the sound of Gary's car in the driveway. He entered through the kitchen door and looked worse than he looked this morning. "Hi, honey," he said in a tired voice.

"Hi, honey, are you okay? You look exhausted." She gave him a hug and was surprised to see how little energy he had.

"I think I caught a bug or something. I am so drained; I have no energy left. Everyone was telling me to go home at lunch, but I just wanted to finish the day since I knew it would be difficult to find a substitute on such short notice. Maybe that was a mistake. I'm sure after a good night sleep, I'll feel better tomorrow. I'm going to head up to bed now. That okay with you?" Meryl checked again to see if her husband was feverish, and there was still no sign of one. She watched him talk with Charlie as he passed through the living room, and decided she'd check on him later.

After watching his show, Charlie came into the kitchen where his mom was preparing dinner. "So Dad isn't feeling well and I need to toss the baseball around. Want to catch with me in the backyard, Mom?" For Charlie to ask her to play catch, she knew he was desperate! He knows she doesn't like playing catch because if she misses the ball, she could get hurt. That's why she wears an umpire's mask... just in case. It's embarrassing for Charlie, a necessity for mom!

"I'm making dinner now. How about going outside and playing basketball? At least you'll be getting exercise," she suggested and used dinner as an excuse. He wasn't happy with the idea but realized he had no other option and grabbed the basketball on his way out the door. A few minutes later Charlie was back, exchanging the basketball for his baseball mitt, his dad's mitt and a baseball.

"What are you doing? Who'd you find to play ball with?" Mom was pleasantly surprised.

"Mr. Vento was outside working, and I asked him if he would play catch with me, and he said he would. He just needs to use dad's mitt," and out he went, slamming the door behind him.

"Thank God for Mr. Vento," Meryl thought to herself.

Chapter Four

"Gary, we really should take you to the doctor. You're barely functioning at work. You've been exhausted every day and can't seem to get your strength back. You have no fever, but maybe it's a nasty case of the flu or something," Meryl didn't like seeing her husband sick, and Gary loathed going to a doctor.

"I think I just strained my whole body the last time we worked outside in the yard," he said, trying to justify his symptoms.

"That was almost two weeks ago! Something isn't right. I've noticed your loss of energy over the past few weeks, but this is much worse. I'm scheduling an appointment for you tomorrow." She left the bedroom. Gary knew better than to argue when she used that tone, and deep down he knew his wife was right. He made himself comfortable and fell back asleep.

Meryl was on the phone making arrangements with the doctor's office when Charlie came home from school. "Hey Mom, I'm home," she could hear from the kitchen.

"In here, Charlie," she replied. "Great, tomorrow at 10 a.m. with Dr. Tadkin. Thank you, good-bye." Meryl hung up the phone.

Charlie walked in at the end of the conversation. "What's going on? Is Dad finally going to the doctor?" Not letting his mom answer, he continued, "That'll be good; they'll give him some medicine and make him feel better." His mom smiled and gave him a hug and kiss hello. She was distracted today. With nothing baking in the oven, Charlie grabbed a bag of snacks and headed to the TV set.

Meryl didn't think to ask about Charlie's day. She just watched him settle in to his routine as her concern for her husband's illness dominated her thoughts. This was a different type of illness that neither one of them has seen before. *"Maybe it's Mono., or the flu, or some other crazy virus that's always going around,"* she thought. She looked forward to hearing what the doctor would say tomorrow, encouraged that the mystery would then be solved.

"How long did the doctor say before we would get the test results back?" Gary asked Meryl as they headed to their favorite restaurant for lunch. Since he took the day off from work, Gary and his wife decided to treat themselves to a date.

"Three days," Meryl said as she recalled the whole appointment. It was good to have someone ask the important questions: "How long have you been feeling tired?" or "I notice a change in the color of your face. Did you notice that lately?" or "You look like you've lost weight. How's your appetite?" It made Gary and Meryl think about the answers and hopefully gave the doctor a clear picture with all of the facts. It was then that they realized this illness didn't come on suddenly; it has existed longer than they initially thought. The two were confident the doctor will have fewer questions and more answers in three days.

Chapter Five

Charlie was doing his homework and Meryl was cooking dinner when the phone rang. Gary picked up the phone.

"Hello, Dr. Tadkin, I wasn't planning on hearing from you for another day or two. Did the tests find anything?" Gary was obviously surprised to hear from the doctor.

All Charlie and Meryl heard was, "Wait, what?... Are you sure?... But I don't understand, I feel fine except for being a little tired. Could there be a mistake?... Okay... tomorrow at nine. We'll see you then." He slowly hung up the phone and, with fear in his eyes, looked at his wife and went upstairs.

"Mom?" Charlie asked, "What's going on? Dad looked freaked out."

"I'm not quite sure, Sweetie. I'll go talk with him. I'll be right back; just keep working on your homework." There was concern in her voice.

When Meryl opened the bedroom door, she found her husband sitting on the bed, staring at his feet, and tears running down his cheeks.

"Gary, what is going on? What did Dr. Tadkin say?" She felt her world unraveling.

She sat down beside him, holding his hand. He looked deep into her eyes and said, "I have cancer, pancreatic cancer. It doesn't look good, and he wants to talk with us tomorrow morning about our options."

"What???.... Oh, Gary..." She wrapped her arms around him as he wept on her shoulder, and she wept along with her husband. The tears seemed to flow freely and endlessly. Gary and his wife cried together in the stillness of their bedroom.

"I don't understand how this could be. I'm scared, Meryl. What if I die? What about you and Charlie? I'm not ready to go yet. I haven't finished the task God has given me." She listened to her husband's worries and concerns.

"What task has God given you that you feel you haven't finished?" She was surprised that this was something weighing heavily on his mind, enough to discuss it at such a time.

"I haven't accomplished being the best husband and father!" he sobbed. "We're supposed to grow old together, retire at the beach and watch the sun set every night. Charlie is still such a young boy. I want to see him grow up to be a man. I want to teach him how to drive, see him graduate high school and college, be independent and work on his own, get married and have children. God's robbing me of this and that's not right; that's not right! How could He do this to one of His children?"

Meryl could see how quickly her husband was heading down the road of despair and anger. Despite her own fear, she tried to comfort him. "First of all, we don't know any details. You already have yourself dead, and there is just too much to live for right now. We need to take one day at a time and hear what the doctor says tomorrow. Our plans might take a detour, but we don't know where the path will lead. This is the part of faith called trust, Gary. Trust in Him and His ways, and we'll be all right."

This new discovery of Gary's health was all very scary for both of them, yet they knew they needed to be strong for their son. They agreed Charlie did not need to know specific details at this moment as there was no need to concern him. Meryl went down to finish preparing dinner, and Gary joined them shortly.

"What's up with Dad? What'd the doctor say?" Charlie asked when his mom reappeared in the kitchen.

"We have to meet with the doctor tomorrow to talk about the test results, and get more information." She made sure she didn't make eye contact with Charlie so he couldn't see the worry on her face or her puffy eyes.

"Okay. When is dinner going to be ready? I'm starving." Meryl silently appreciated the innocence of Charlie being eleven at this moment, as even she heard Charlie's stomach rumble from a few feet away.

"It'll be ready in about a half-an-hour. Why not grab an apple, then play outside for awhile? That'll keep your mind off of your tummy." She tossed Charlie an apple. As soon as Charlie was out the door, Meryl turned around, faced the stove and let out a deep, guttural sigh. These next few weeks were not going to be easy for the Nelson family.

Chapter Six

With Gary at work and Charlie at school, Meryl decided to return Mr. Vento's brownie plate, hoping that the two of them would be able to talk. As she reached to press the doorbell, the front door swung open.

"Hi, Meryl. Oh, you didn't have to return the plate. I forgot all about it." His happy face quickly turned to one of concern.

"What's the matter? Please come in and sit down." He motioned her into the living room.

Meryl could barely speak a word before beginning to cry. Over the past few weeks, Mr. Vento had a feeling something was wrong, because he hadn't seen anyone outside playing with Charlie. He wanted to give the family their privacy. He figured, if they wanted him to know anything, they would tell him.

An hour later, Meryl thanked Dominic for the tea and the talk, and headed back home. She was so appreciative that Mr. Vento was there to listen and offer comfort. He offered to help with cooking, driving to the doctor and watching Charlie. The Nelson's knew help was only a driveway away, day or night. And for that, they all were appreciative.

Gary was due to arrive shortly since he was now only working half-days. He had another doctor's appointment this afternoon. Gary wanted to finish the school year, which was only a few weeks away. The days were getting harder and harder to endure, since he was first diagnosed a month ago. His body was so tired; he really had no strength. The family was looking forward to the summer, to let Gary's body rest and regain some much needed energy.

When Gary came home, Meryl explained how she met with Dominic and that he had offered to watch Charlie while they were at the doctor. Gary was appreciative to have such a caring neighbor.

During the car ride to the appointment, Meryl made a difficult suggestion, but one that needed to be said. "Gary, I was thinking that since your energy level is so low right now, what if we find you a temporary replacement to coach Charlie's baseball team? Just until you feel better. That way, it won't be a strain on the other two coaches, and you won't feel bad about not being able to help." She kept looking ahead as she drove and waited to hear the response. Meryl knew how much coaching meant to Gary and the joy he felt watching the boys play. This illness seemed to be taking away this joy. "Why not ask my brother, Pete?" she continued since there was no reaction coming from her husband, and the silence was deafening. "I'm sure he wouldn't mind, and since he lives nearby it wouldn't be that much of an inconvenience. I know the other coaches would understand and would welcome any additional help." Still, there was silence. "*What is going through his mind?*" she wondered.

As they neared the building of the doctor's office, Gary broke down. "This is unbelievable that you would ask me such a thing. How could you ask me to give up coaching my son's baseball team? A team I have coached for years, with many of the same kids. I don't care if I am too weak to stand; I will sit in a chair by the sidelines. I can coach from a chair; my voice can carry. Don't ask me to give that up, Meryl. Please, don't. I'm not dead, you know."

Gary was unable to see the tears welling up in his wife's eyes as she continued to stare at the road ahead. Meryl felt so deeply wounded as she then realized the severity that this diagnosis has brought to their family, not only regarding the health of her husband but of the emotions that have stirred within all of them. For her particularly, she didn't want people to see her husband struggle or become weaker. She even tried to shield Charlie from what was so clearly obvious. She tried to reason that just as the adults must adjust and cope, Charlie must try to do the same, that the three of them needed to understand and accept the new terms of their family's life. She tried to convince herself that words may not need to be spoken to Charlie, who would eventually see and understand the gradual way his dad's illness would dictate their daily life. Meryl was really struggling to come to terms with all of this.

"We're here. Do you want me to drive you to the front door?" she asked.

"No, that's okay. Just walk slowly with me, all right?" Gary asked, as he reached to hold her hand.

How quickly their life was changing. Even the smallest, seemingly meaningless aspects of ordinary life have now come into focus. For as long as she could remember, Gary *always* walked faster and ahead of Meryl. He would normally have to slow down and wait for her. And yet, here they were now, with Gary walking at a much slower pace, which just happened to be Meryl's usual walking speed. Since they were now walking hand in hand, Meryl couldn't help but reflect, *"Is this a gift, a blessing in disguise?"*

Hours later, they both walked in to a house where it looked like a meal was in the making: dinner cooking in the oven, the aroma of warming bread, and fixings for ice cream sundaes on the kitchen counter. What a contrast to the environment from where Meryl and Gary had just left. A sterile, antiseptic doctor's office, where the fear of death loomed and helplessness abounded, to this welcoming, comforting site. Mr. Vento was at the stove wearing Meryl's big red apron, the one that read, "Kiss the Cook!", and normally wrapped twice around her waist, but seemed to fit Dominic just fine! It was a pleasure and relief to be greeted by the smile and the warmth of the homey atmosphere.

"Hey, look who's home, Charlie!" Mr. Vento said with his usual positive, uplifting tone. Dominic gave Meryl a hug hello then took her coat. He shook Gary's hand and said, "Good to see you, Buddy. Here, let me take that for you." Mr. Vento helped Gary remove his coat and then hung both coats in the closet.

As Charlie entered the kitchen, he was full of questions. "Hey, Mom; hey, Dad. What happened at the doctor's? What'd you find out?"

"We'll talk about it over dinner," Meryl said,

as she rubbed the temples of her forehead.

Mr. Vento could see that Meryl needed a break, so he suggested, "You know what, Meryl, why don't you have a seat in the living room? I'll put on some tea for you while you relax with your boy. I'll call you when it's ready." Meryl was so mentally drained that she didn't hesitate to take him up on his offer.

Even though Gary was impressed with how well Mr. Vento seemed to have the Nelson's kitchen under control, he was overwhelmed with the conflict of seeing someone in his home caring for him and his family. He just couldn't shake the thoughts of wanting to be the strong one, that he should be helping with the cooking; he should be the one greeting Mr. Vento at the door, not the other way around. It made him feel very vulnerable, allowing Mr. Vento to reverse the roles and take over. But before Gary's thoughts continued on the path toward self-pity and shame, Dominic placed a cutting board, knife, peeler and a bunch of carrots in front of him.

"I could use an extra pair of hands here; can you help me?" Dominic asked as he placed the bowl next to the cutting board. Gary knew the carrots were not a necessity and clearly understood Dominic's motive. He may be sick, but he is not useless. He did not want to be a burden and did not want to feel as one. Gary recognized that his friend appreciated all he had to offer, whether a lot or a little; they were just thankful for the time they spent together.

"I would love to help you; thanks for asking," Gary said. As he started working on the carrots, Gary talked to Dominic about the doctor's visit and that it didn't look like there were many options. He shared how they were seeking the advice of a specialist and expressed his desire of meeting with the specialist sooner rather than later. Dominic was sorry to hear the latest news and said he would ask a friend of his, who's brother happened to be going through a similar situation, about resources and offered to put the two men in touch with one another. He offered that he thought it might be comforting to talk with someone in a similar situation, for Gary to realize that he wasn't alone in his struggle, and that no matter what Gary's situation brought, perhaps he would find consolation in sharing his situation with someone else in similar circumstances.

Charlie was teaching his mom how to work the controller for one of his favorite videogames. He kept beating her because she didn't have any idea of how the thing worked! But she was enjoying spending the time with her son, something that was happening less and less these days. More of Meryl's attention had been focused on her husband and the needs around his illness. She tried to remember that her son had needs, too. She and

Charlie found laughter through her gaming inexperience, causing her defeat by thousands of points.

"Look, I'm pressing this button to walk straight, and it's turning me around! Why do I keep going the wrong way?" she asked as she pointed to the game controller. When the call for dinner was heard, Mom demanded a re-match in the near future!

At the dinner table, the four of them discussed the doctor's visit in very simple terms. They talked about finding a specialist and what benefits a specialist could offer. Since there was nothing that could be done tonight, everyone promised to enjoy the dinner and the company of each other. The topic of baseball and Charlie's team was raised. Meryl spoke of her concern for Gary being unable to coach effectively due to his physical weakness.

That's when Mr. Vento offered, "I can help. I'm right next door, so how about if I drive the two of you to games and practices? Gary, I can borrow your mitt, or I could just buy a new one. You know, I try to attend many of Charlie's games anyway, so it's just a few extra practices, and there are other coaches to help. What is it my mother used to say, "More hands make light work?" This will be fun. It's been many years since I've been a baseball coach, but I'm sure the fundamentals haven't changed! I just have to brush up on the rules. And anyway, you'll be the brains," he said as he pointed to Gary, "and I'll be the brute!" He flexed both of his arm muscles which made everyone laugh!

"Yeah, come on, Dad, that'd be fun having Mr. Vento as a coach. We'll call him Coach V for short. My friends will love him."

Gary felt at a loss for words, so he agreed, "If you're sure you wouldn't mind, I'd love it if you joined us." Those feelings of vulnerability and guilt were rising again...

"Oh, this is great! I know you're in the middle of the season, so what's the team's record? When's the next practice? Who are we playing against next?" Mr. Vento's excitement was so evident that Gary let his own anxiety disappear. Gary could see how this might be fun!

Conversation about baseball turned in to Charlie sharing what happened at school that day, which prompted his dad to share what happened at school, and then continued with Mr. Vento recalling memories from years ago. He shared the story of when he was a young boy, playing baseball with his older brother. Apparently, Dominic was always the smallest and the fastest of the group. One day, the boys were playing stick ball in the apartment lined street. Standing on the first step of a stoop (a make-shift first base), he was the winning run with two outs. His older brother wanted an older kid to pinch run for Dominic, but Dominic would not leave first base.

So his brother told him, "When I hit it, RUN! You understand Dominic, RUN!"

"Wight Johnny, wun!" Dominic imitated how he spoke as a young boy.

Johnny, a big kid for his age, who was nicknamed "Johnny Juice" because he always hit well in a squeeze, stepped up to the plate. The entire outfield backed up. The pitcher threw his hardest fast ball down the middle and BAM! Johnny Juice hit it with all his might. When he saw his brother hit the ball, Dominic took off running, just like his big brother told him. He was so focused on running home and winning the game for the team that he didn't realize the ball had shattered Mrs. Spina's third floor bedroom window.

By the time he jumped up and down on home plate yelling "I did it, I did it!" Mrs. Spina was yelling through her broken window, "Since you did it, Dominic Vento, you will pay for it. I'm telling your parents!"

Dominic stood in stunned silence as he looked around for his older brother to accept the blame. He was shocked when he saw that the field was empty. What was, a few moments ago, alive with the energy of a dozen adrenaline-pumped boys, was now vacant and deserted.

Dominic stood in the middle of the road oblivious to a car coming from behind and honking for him to get out of the way. He couldn't believe everyone left! It took Dominic months to work off the expense to replace the window, and he didn't talk to his brother for a long time after that. The Nelson's always enjoyed Mr. Vento's childhood stories. Life seemed much simpler then…

Chapter Seven

"Play ball!" the umpire announced. On this beautifully sunny day in June, Charlie's team was the home team. They took the field first, with their red shirts, white pants and blue hats. The winning team will be the town champs and receive trophies and accolades. Mr. Vento had been working with the team for a month now and had gotten to know the other coaches and the strengths and weaknesses of each player. He stood beside Gary, who was seated in the dugout where he could see everyone in position on the field. Mr. Vento learned how to record the game in the scorebook, a job no other coach welcomed. He actually enjoyed having to do it because it forced him to continuously pay attention to the game. Before each inning, Charlie's dad spoke with each boy about their game. He was feeling very much a part of the team.

The game was tied at the final inning. Charlie's team was last to bat. The atmosphere was charged with anticipation, and Charlie's mom watched from the crowded stands. There were coaches and players from other teams watching the game. The bench was cheering each player that stepped up to the plate. The first player struck out. The second player popped out. Next in the line up was Charlie. To the plate he walked, with two outs and a tie game. The pressure was on… Charlie could continue the game or end it.

Mr. Vento leapt up from his seat and called, "Time!" A month ago, he wouldn't have had the courage to do that, but today he felt like he was watching his grandson play. He felt like a member of the team. As he walked toward Charlie at the plate, the three other coaches looked at each other and smiled because they realized how out of character it was for Coach V to have such confidence. Mr. Vento usually asked permission from the other coaches before doing any thing! Gary and Meryl gave each other a smile. No one knew what Coach V said to Charlie and frankly, no one cared; they knew he was guiding Charlie with the best baseball wisdom that he could summon.

When Coach V returned to the dugout, Gary asked, "What'd you tell him?" Charlie's dad was expecting to hear some great words of inspiration or precise baseball strategy. Coach V replied, as he looked out to the pitcher's mound, "I asked him what his favorite ice cream flavor is." Puzzled, Gary looked at Dominic's profile and asked,

"What?" Coach V repeated, "I asked him what his favorite ice cream flavor is, because I'm sure he's all nervous inside. So I wanted to distract him. I wanted him to focus on something else for a second. I also told him whether we win or lose, I'll treat the team to ice cream after the game." Dominic turned to Gary and smiled.

"Ball!"

"Ball!"

"Strike!"

"Strike!"

"Ball!"

Every body was nervous. "Come on, Charlie, full count. Show us what you've got," one of Charlie's coaches yelled from the third base line. The pitcher got set, threw the pitch, and Charlie swung.

Charlie nailed it, right down the middle! "Run, Charlie, run!" his teammates roared. Every one was jumping up and down and screaming from the bleachers. The first base coach sent him to second. Will the throw from center field beat Charlie to second??? Oh, this was nerve-wracking! Charlie slid under the tag and was "SAFE!" The bench was screaming and the parents started to cheer the next batter.

"Come on, Thomas, get a hit!" was heard from the dugout and the stands.

Before Thomas left the dug out, Coach V asked him, "So, Thomas, what's your favorite movie?" Thomas walked backward toward home plate as he shouted his answer. Coach V shook his head up and down as he returned to the dugout.

"I haven't seen that one; I'll have to go see it." Dominic looked at Gary, who was chuckling, and said, "Hey, it worked with Charlie!" Gary agreed.

"Strike!"

"Ball!"

Thomas planted his feet and watched the next pitch come in. He read the pitch and swung.

"Strike!"

"Shoot," he said to himself, and he started his routine again: get set; plant feet; bat back. He heard Charlie, from second, yell, "Come on, Tom, hit me in. Hit me in, Tom." The pitcher went in to motion, released the ball with the fastest speed Tom had seen yet, and Tom went for it. He swung like he'd never swung before!

Tom hit the ball down the first base line. As Tom ran towards first, the third base coach waved Charlie home. Charlie knew this was it; Tom knew this was it; everybody in the dugout and in the bleachers knew this was it! Charlie had to be safe; Tom had to be safe. The throw went straight over the first baseman's head, aimed for the catcher who braced himself for a close play at home. The umpire positioned himself so he could make a good call. The catcher caught the ball a few feet above the plate, and that gave Charlie just a split-second to slide under and touch home plate.

"SAFE!" was all they needed to hear. The boys emptied the dugout and piled on top of Charlie! What a thrill for the home team! For many of them, this was the first time they'd been on a championship team. The coaches hugged each other, and the parents celebrated in the stands. It was a great game, and the makings of a great memory.

Chapter Eight

Charlie walked ever so slowly out of Lincoln Elementary on the last day of school. He ran his fingers along the bumpy hallway walls of cream painted cement blocks, past the principal's office, past the nurse's office to the door outside. He stared at where the buses waited in the circle, a site he'd seen over and over but just never really noticed. He said good-bye to the principal, Mrs. Sullivan, who gave him a hug and wished him luck in middle school. She told Charlie to have his dad stay in touch with her over the summer. Charlie walked along the sidewalk and before turning the corner, he looked at the school one last time and thought, *"There is no turning back now."*

During the walk home, Charlie's mood quickly changed from sadness to excitement. As soon as the school was out of sight, he realized, "NO SCHOOL OVER THE SUMMER! No studying, no homework, just fun, fun, fun!" Charlie rounded the corner and as he passed Mr. Vento's house, he noticed the car carrier attached to the roof of his family's car. *"What's going on?"* Charlie searched his mind... He ran into the house and tripped over the suitcases that were piled in the middle of the floor. His mom came running in to the living room to see if he was hurt. Charlie had forgotten all about his family's annual summer vacation to Cape May. They had spoken about it over the past months but Charlie had been distracted with the thoughts about leaving elementary school, entering middle school and his father's health, that it was such a great surprise when he realized they were leaving tomorrow for New Jersey.

"Charlie, are you all right?" his mom asked as she helped him up.

"Yeah, Mom, I'm fine. What time are we leaving? I still have to pack," Charlie said as he grabbed one of the empty suitcases he just fell over and started heading up to his room.

"We're leaving tomorrow morning," she yelled up the stairs towards the direction of his room. She smiled as she heard the slamming of dresser drawers. Over the past five years, Meryl had seen how much her son has enjoyed staying at their favorite beach house near Sunset Beach, biking down Beach Avenue and riding the waves along the Jersey shore. She also knew this vacation would be unlike any other. It could be the last time all three of them vacation together as a family.

"Meryl, is he okay?" She heard from the kitchen.

"Yes, he's fine. He tripped over the suitcases I left out. He's upstairs packing and should be down in a minute. You know how our son packs, quickly and without much thought," she joked as she and her husband continued packing groceries for the vacation.

"Hey, Dad," Charlie said as he kissed both his parents hello. As Gary sat at the kitchen table, he instructed his wife on what and how to pack. Meryl wasn't thrilled with her husband's "suggestions", but she knew her husband well enough to realize how particular he was about the packing process and that he meant no disrespect to her as he handed out orders. She also realized that this was Gary's only way to help, now that the illness kept him tired and incapacitated most of the time.

Charlie was unable to find some snack food that wasn't already packed. "Here," Mom offered a filled brown grocery bag, "you'll find something in there to eat."

"Thanks, I'm starving," Charlie said as he grabbed the grocery bag and pulled out a box of granola bars.

"Soooo… how was it? How was your last day of elementary school, Mister I'm-a big-middle-schooler-now?" his father asked.

"It's weird, Dad. I want to go to middle school because Lincoln seems like such a baby school now that I'm older. But it's scary going to a new school, meeting kids from other elementary schools, not knowing any of the teachers, wondering if I'll have any classes with my friends, having to make new friends. You know..." Charlie munched on his snack and got a drink.

"I know, Charlie. I remember when I went from Flower Hill Elementary to Weber Junior High. They called middle school "junior high" back in the olden days," he smiled at his wife. "And the elementary schools went from kindergarten to sixth grade, junior high was seventh to ninth and high school was tenth to twelfth." Dad continued, "Imagine being a *sixth* grader in an elementary school! I remember the little stairway leading to the music room. I could take four stairs at a time when I was in sixth grade!" He smiled as he reminisced about his younger years. He recalled to himself the time in third grade, when John Hampton refused to enter the classroom and insisted on standing in the hallway. The whole class sat at their desks listening to the teacher as the principal tried to reason with John in the hallway. When the principal came in, with his arms under John's armpits, carrying John as he jumped up and down in a tantrum, we all stared at him till the teacher started talking again. The principal left as quickly as he entered, and that was that! John Hampton was okay, as he sat staring at the top of his desk with his face beet red from crying. And then there was the last day of sixth grade. Ms. Gordon took the whole class on a field trip to the ice cream store down the road. Everyone walked there together, drank ice cream shakes, and walked back to school. Those were good times, Charlie's dad recalled with a smile. He wondered where all of his friends from elementary school were now and what they were doing.

"Gary... Gary, what do you think?" Meryl interrupted his thoughts.

"Huh?" Gary responded, his mind obviously still back in elementary school.

"Do you want two boxes of cereal or three?" she asked for the third time, as she stood there waving the boxes, waiting for his reply.

"Honey, it's only for a week. Two boxes should be plenty for the three of us, don't you think?" he asked, turning to Charlie.

"Yeah, Mom, two is plenty. We'll be going out to Flap Jack's for some chocolate chip pancakes, right?" Charlie said as he raised his eyebrows in anticipation.

"Flap Jack's for breakfast for sure, The Italian Garden for dinner and the Boardwalk for some fried dough and french fries," she said with a yummy smile on her face.

"So, I know what you're saying, Charlie. You feel big enough to move on to an older and bigger school. But you don't know what you're moving to, and that's a little scary," Dad affirmed.

"Yeah, the unknown," Charlie said.

"Yeah, the unknown," his dad repeated. "I know that all too well."

"What about you, Dad? How was your last day of school? I stopped by to give you a cupcake from our class, but Mrs. Hutchinson told me you went home already."

"Well, it was okay. I guess you could say it was weird for me, too. Your mom and I stayed only a few hours, enough to say good-bye to a few teachers, Mrs. Sullivan and a few children that I saw on my way out. I was really tired and drained. I took a nice long nap when I got home, and now I'm feeling refreshed," he said as he gave a happy face, showing that big smile of his. It always made everyone around him smile when he smiled, and this time was no different. Charlie relayed Mrs. Sullivan's message to his dad, who agreed that he would stay in touch with many of the staff members over the summer.

Chapter Nine

The Nelson family looked tan and felt well rested. Every day they went to Sunset Beach or the Beach Avenue beach. It was difficult for Charlie's father to walk on the sand and keep his balance, so they didn't travel too far from the entrance. They enjoyed walking the Washington Street outdoor mall together where they had some great fudge, bought some souvenirs and ate dinner at The Italian Garden. One evening, the three of them rode in a horse and buggy carriage, rambling along the Victorian house-lined streets, where the artistic combination of the three different colored paints, beautiful gardens and inviting front porches with the gingerbread lattice enhanced the neighborhood beauty.

As has been the tradition for the past five years, on the day before they left for home, Charlie and his mom walked the beach at sunrise, from the Cape May Lighthouse to wherever they get tired, then turned around and headed back. Each year, as Charlie got older and stronger, the walk got longer and longer. This year, Meryl, wondered if they would actually be able to walk all the way to the Wildwood boardwalk and back.

"Good morning," his mom gently whispered as she kissed Charlie's cheek, and sat beside him on the bed.

"Time for our mom 'n son walk," she cajoled as she watched for signs of life under the bed covers. She had been looking forward to this walk all week.

"Mom, are you kidding me? The sun isn't even up yet; it can't be time for sunrise. Come back when the sun is up." Charlie threw the covers over his head and didn't move.

"Oh, no you don't!" she peeled back the covers to expose his face. "Come on, Charlie; you, me, the sand, the water, the sea gulls… and maybe even some dolphins. Let's see if we can walk down to Wildwood this year." By now the sun was peeking above the horizon, and the sky was transforming from darkness to beautiful pinks. "Come on Charlie," she said, as she got up. His mom grabbed a pair of jeans and a t-shirt from his dresser, and tossed them on top of his covers. "I'll wait for you outside."

A few minutes later, the front door swung open and a very groggy Charlie, with hair that resembled the blades of a helicopter, appeared with his football. His mom was waiting on the porch bench, holding two sweatshirts, and Meryl smiled as she saw her son. "All set?" she asked as she headed to the car.

"Yep. Wait, I didn't say good-bye to dad; does he know we're leaving?" Charlie asked with half opened eyes.

"I left a note for him on the kitchen table. This week has wiped him out, so he told me last night that he'd love a morning where he can just sleep late. He should be up when we get back," she said.

Chapter Ten

A drive that took twenty minutes at noon, took only five minutes at this time of the day. They parked on Beach Avenue and headed to the shore. Meryl closed her eyes for an instant, to savor this moment of the sea gulls flying over head as the birds scavenged for their breakfast among the remains of low tide, smelling the salt water as the waves crashed ashore and feeling the wind blow against her face and the sand squish between her toes.

Her moment was disrupted when Charlie yelled, "Go long, Mom, go long." He pumped the football, and she ran a few yards further away from him. He threw it against the wind so it landed in front of her. She scooped it up and yelled to her son, "I can't throw it that far; you have to come in closer." Charlie ran towards her, and she threw the football the best she could. Her attempt caused the two of them to chuckle! As they played catch, an older couple walked hand in hand along the water's edge, with their pants cuffed. A dog played catch with its owner, and there were a few joggers plugged in to their ear buds, who either smiled or paid no attention to those who passed. Every so often they saw a beautiful shell or a horseshoe crab or a jellyfish. It was serene, peaceful, just mom and her son. It felt like a stark contrast to the stresses of their family life over the past few months. Charlie's mom decided to take this opportunity to talk with Charlie about what they've been going through.

"You have a good time this week, Charlie?" she asked.

"Yeah, I love it down here. I love the beach," he replied.

"What was your favorite thing we did this week?" she wondered.

After quite a long pause, Charlie answered, "I really liked Wildwood. The Boardwalk was great, and it was so cool to win a prize! It was fun racing you and Dad in the race cars." The smile remained on his face.

"You think your dad had a good time this week?" Meryl continued to walk down the beach, her eyes focused on the sand below.

"I don't know, I guess so. He got to feel the water on his feet, he has a nice tan, and he laughed a lot." Charlie looked inland at the many beachfront hotels.

"Did you enjoy Cape May more this year or last year?" Meryl asked.

"I kind of liked it better last year. I mean, it was still a lot of fun this year, but it's just different now, that's all," Charlie answered.

"What do you mean by different?" His mom pressed on.

"I don't know. I can't really explain it." Charlie was feeling uncomfortable.

"Then don't try to explain it. Just say it." Meryl was trying to understand what her son was feeling.

"Dad was such a pain sometimes," he blurted out. This comment really caught Meryl by surprise, but she took in a deep breath of that beach air and continued looking straight ahead as they walked.

"He was such a pain because... he didn't want to do what you wanted to do sometimes?" She decided to start asking questions in the hopes that Charlie would further explain himself.

"No, it wasn't that."

"He was such a pain because... he was crabby sometimes?" She was really trying to help her son sort this out.

"No..., well yeah, he was crabby sometimes. But it's not really that." Charlie was not making this any easier.

"Okay, Charlie, what then? I think you know. Just say it." She was starting to lose her patience but was careful to stay in control. She wanted to make sure that her son had a safe place to express himself.

"Promise you won't get mad or anything?" Charlie asked.

"Charlie, I'll only get mad if you aren't honest with me. Why do you feel your dad was a pain?" With this, she stopped and faced her son.

"It's just that it's like having a baby brother around. He needs help when he walks. He can't walk that far, so we have to take breaks or change our plans. We do things around his nap schedule. It always seems to be time for medicine. I just wish I had the Dad from last year who would ride the waves with me, play football with me on the beach, take care of *me*. Now *I* take care of *him*. Do you know this is the first time I took this football to the beach this week!" He shoved the football in his mom's arms and broke down crying, his knees buckling and dropping to the sand. "I miss him, Mom. I miss my dad."

"I miss him too, Charlie. I miss your dad, and I miss my husband," she admitted quietly as she, too, dropped to the ground and embraced her son. She stared out to the horizon, wondering what the future held for her family.

Chapter Eleven

Gary was thrilled to see his house in the distance. The time spent in Cape May was not as enjoyable as he hoped. During the vacation, he felt like a burden to Meryl and a disappointment to Charlie. Neither Meryl nor Charlie complained, but Gary was surprised to see how much he relied on them to help him walk or wait on him. During the car ride home, he remembered that Charlie didn't even ask to play catch on the beach or bike to Sunset Beach like they had done in the past. He assumed his son realized he could not physically do these things, so didn't bother to ask. This discouraging thought was on his mind as they pulled in to their driveway.

Mr. Vento appeared, excited as ever, "Boy, did I miss you guys!" he said. He greeted everyone with a big hug and kiss.

"Hi, Dominic. Anything exciting happen on the block last week?" Meryl asked as she reached to pull the luggage from the rooftop car carrier. She handed Charlie his luggage, and he quickly ran off to play videogames and call a few friends.

"No, it was pretty quiet here, too quiet without you guys around." He helped Meryl with the luggage and brought a few bags in to the house. "Did you have a nice time, Gary?" He looked at Charlie's dad, who seemed a little sad.

"It was a nice time, Dominic," Gary tried to sound convincing. "Beautiful weather, I got a nice tan and we shared some memories. I just need to rest for a little while. Honey, do you mind if I lie down for a bit?" Gary looked at Meryl.

"No, don't worry about this. We'll put the bags in the rooms and you can take care of your luggage later. Do you need anything?" Meryl got used to always adding this question at the end of whatever she said.

"No, I'm good. Dominic, I'll see you later." Gary started walking towards the house.

"All right," Dominic said. Before Gary reached the house, Dominic asked, "Hey, how about if everyone comes over to my house for dinner tonight? I know you don't have any groceries in your house after being gone for a week, so what do you say?" Dominic looked at Meryl and then Gary who, without hesitation, welcomed the invitation.

With Gary inside, Dominic talked with Meryl, "Are you doing okay? I can see Gary isn't doing as well as even a week ago. Do you need some extra help? I'd be happy to help you, you know that, right?"

Mr. Vento reminded Meryl of her father, which is why she always felt comfortable around him. He often told her she was the daughter he and his wife never had. Their relationship seemed so comfortable, so familiar, that Dominic instinctively knew when something was bothering her. He knew that today, Meryl was even more stressed than usual, which wasn't a good sign especially just after being "on vacation" for a week.

It was because of this relationship that Meryl was able to honestly answer, "No, Dominic; no, I'm not doing okay," she could feel the tears fill her eyes. She kept busy by unloading the car, only so she wouldn't break down right there on the driveway. "My husband is getting weaker by the day; Charlie misses the way his father was just six months ago; I miss the way my husband was six months ago. I just want life to stand still for a moment, because everything is changing so rapidly. It's just so overwhelming."

Dominic took Meryl by the shoulders so she would stop moving, and looked at her with determination in his eyes, "You're going to get through this. We are all in this together – you, me, Gary, Charlie, all of us. You are not alone, and you're going to be okay." He hugged her as she placed her head on his shoulders and wept.

On his way to the bedroom, Gary passed a window which overlooked the driveway. He watched Dominic consoling Meryl, who was obviously upset. Gary felt the devastating effects this illness was having on not only himself, but on his son and his wife. He cried, alone, in the silence of his bedroom.

Chapter Twelve

With the passing of each July and August day, the Nelson family created and stored more memories. Mr. Vento checked in on the family daily to see how he could help. One day he ran a few errands for Meryl; another day he spent hanging out with Charlie; another day, he sat with Gary while Meryl and Charlie were able to have some time together. He was truly part of this family, and the Nelson's could not have managed without his help.

One hot and humid August Saturday, Gary and Dominic sat enjoying a cold glass of orange juice when Gary decided it was time to express his gratitude towards his friend. As they sat in the living room making small talk, Gary took a deep sigh, "Dominic...," they made eye contact. "I want to thank you for helping us out and going beyond the call of duty as a neighbor. You are such a great help to me and my family. I will always be grateful." Gary stopped, but Dominic sensed he wasn't finished. With tears in his eyes, Gary stared at Dominic and said, "Please help them when I'm gone. I know how much each of them is fond of you, and it would ease my nerves if I knew they could look to you for help. I don't want this to be a burden for you; it's just so hard for me to know I won't be here to protect them and take care of them. Just… whatever you have to offer them, I would appreciate it." Gary looked down into his lap as the tears streamed down his face.

Dominic reassured him, "Gary… you, Meryl and Charlie are my family, and I love you like you were my own. Try not to worry. Just enjoy this time and treasure every moment. I'm not going anywhere, and Meryl knows that. Right now, we're focusing on you and making you comfortable. Leave the rest to us." Dominic walked over to Gary and placed his hand on Gary's shoulder. Gary placed his hand over Dominic's.

"We're home!" Charlie's shout from the kitchen broke the somber moment. Gary exchanged a glance with Dominic, as if to say, "thank you", and he patted his friend's hand. Dominic squeezed Gary's shoulder as a sign of reassurance and compassion, and then he walked in to the bustling kitchen. Charlie and his mom had gone grocery shopping, and the kitchen floor was covered with bags of food: cereal boxes, meats for dinner, snacks, bottles of juice and water, fruits and vegetables.

Mr. Vento helped carry the food from the car. After greeting her husband, Meryl stocked the cabinets and Charlie stayed with his dad.

"Hey, Pop!" Charlie plopped on to the sofa, "What are you doing?"

Gary couldn't help but laugh because he wasn't able to do much these days except sit, eat and sleep. "Nothing much," he replied. "What are you doing?" he asked.

"Nothing really. I wanted to talk to you about mom's birthday; it's coming up, you know," he whispered. Panic struck Gary's face! From his reaction, it was obvious he had forgotten his wife's birthday.

"Charlie, what's today's date?" his dad asked quickly to see how much time he had left to figure out what to do. He needed to know if the birthday was this week, next week, when?

"Today is August 25th," Charlie whispered.

Gary regained his composure as he slowly calculated. "Good. We still have about a week to plan something for your mom. Charlie, I really want to do something special for her this year. She deserves the best. Thank goodness you said something. What would I do without you?" His dad proudly looked at Charlie, which made his son feel special.

Charlie smiled and jokingly said, "You're one lucky Dad, aren't you?"

"I sure am, son. I sure am. I'm very, very blessed," he truthfully admitted.

Chapter Thirteen

Gary hollered for Mr. Vento to join them in the living room, to plan a party for Meryl. She knew something was stirring when she entered the room and all discussion stopped, three pairs of eyes staring at her and guilty expressions on all three faces! "What's going on?" she asked curiously.

"Nothing," was said by all three males at the same time.

"Really?" she said, not believing them.

"Yep. Nothing at all, Meryl." Gary assumed leadership of the three liars.

"Okay." All six eyes followed her as she walked through the living room, heading toward the stairs. One by one, she stared at them. "When you're finished doing nothing, let me know and I'll start dinner."

"Okay, thanks, Honey." Gary looked at the other two, and she could hear the three of them laughing as she headed up the stairs. She smiled because laughter wasn't happening as much in this house lately, and at this moment, it sure was music to her ears.

The three men talked about having a big birthday party in a restaurant with family and friends, or maybe a small party at home with just the four of them; what her favorite meal was; what gifts they should get, all the decisions that had to be made. They decided on the small home party, and Dominic and Gary decided to go shopping after Gary's doctor's appointment tomorrow. Charlie was in charge of keeping his mom occupied while Gary found the perfect gift. There was a lot of planning, shopping and decorating to do but not much time to do it. Yet, all were up for the challenge, especially Gary. He wanted to make this a special birthday, one his wife would never forget, since he knew there was a good chance it could be the last time he would celebrate her birthday.

Chapter Fourteen

Meryl woke up early on the morning of her birthday. During the past few days, neither Gary nor Charlie had given her any hint that they remembered it was her day. In fact, she purposely dropped a few hints, but neither of them seemed to take the bait. Meryl glanced over at her husband who lied beside her. He looked so peaceful just lying there; she could smell his cologne, see the stubble on his thinner face and then, that big wide grin began to emerge.

"Hey, I thought you were sleeping," she whispered as she kissed her husband good morning.

"Good morning, Birthday Girl," he said, which brought a big smile to her face. The past few weeks have been so hard to keep the many secrets from her!

"I thought everyone forgot; no one said a word. Does Charlie know?" she asked curiously.

"Oh, I think so," Gary replied, as he reached over to his nightstand to retrieve an envelope from the drawer. He handed it to her. "Happy Birthday, Honey."

It was a plain white envelope with her name written on it. Inside was a gift certificate for a "Day of Beauty" from the spa in town. Gary thought she should start her birthday celebration with a massage, manicure and pedicure. The spa served two purposes: most importantly, his wife would get some much deserved pampering. And secondly, while she was out of the house, the three guys would have time to decorate and prepare for the party. Meryl was thrilled at the thought of a few hours of pampering.

"I made your appointment for eleven o'clock, so after your massage, you can have lunch and then get your nails done," Gary said proudly. He really did put a lot of thought in to this and she realized it.

"I love you," she snuggled into the arms of her husband.

"I love you, too," he said, giving her as strong of a hug as he could.

Just then their bedroom door flew open. "You two up yet?" Charlie yelled and jumped on the bed right in between his parents. "Happy Birthday, Mom!" he said as he leaned over and kissed her cheek.

"Thanks, Sweetie! You and Dad had me going there. I thought you both forgot. You didn't give away one clue," Charlie's mom was so impressed with their secrecy.

Looking at his dad, Charlie asked, "So, did you give it to her yet?"

"Yes, he did," Charlie's mom said, "and I love it!"

Looking at his father, Charlie continued, "Did you show her what was written on the inside?"

"What are you talking about, Charlie? Of course I saw what was written on the inside! I ripped the envelope open! I knew it had to be something special." His mom thought Charlie lost his mind! Her son turned around and saw she was holding an envelope.

Charlie's dad seemed to speak to him in code when he said, "Charlie has to get going now. His room needs cleaning." He waved him out of the room in an effort to get him to leave.

Charlie kept talking as he walked backwards towards the doorway. "What is going on? I'm confused." Charlie talked back to his dad in the same monotonous code-like manner. Meryl looked very strangely at both of them.

His dad, who was still in bed, continued to speak slowly to Charlie, "She loved her day-at-the-spa gift!" As Charlie stopped to ask his dad a question, his mom shook her head in bewilderment and headed to the bathroom to get ready for her big day.

"What are you talking about? What "day-at-the-spa"? Didn't you give her the ring? I thought you were going to give her the ring first thing. What happened?" Charlie had no idea the plans had changed.

"Shhhhh," his dad whispered, "she'll hear you. I came up with the idea about the day at the spa so she'll be out of the house while we're getting ready for the party. I'll give her the ring later." Pointing to his brain, he added, "You've got one smart dad, don't cha'? Come on, don't cha'?" His dad started rough housing with him on the bed. It was nice for Charlie to catch a glimpse of how his dad used to be. He missed times like these.

Chapter Fifteen

As soon as Mr. Vento saw Meryl leave the house, he ran over with the decorations. They knew they had only a few hours and needed to make the most of it. Gary took the decorations into the dining room, while Dominic helped Charlie bake a cake. All three still needed to wrap their presents and shop for her favorite dinner.

"Wait till mom sees this!" Charlie exclaimed, "She'll be so surprised." He quickly got the cake mix, cake pan and mixing bowls from the cupboard. He knew where everything was from watching or helping his mom make dozens of cupcakes over the years.

"It was so hard keeping this from her all week," Mr. Vento admitted as he got the ingredients and followed Charlie's lead.

"I can't tell you how many times I almost slipped," Gary said, coming in from the dining room. He was able to hang a decoration or two, but the commotion and the effort was really tiring him out. He decided to sit in the kitchen and watch the birthday cake get made. The three of them decided that after the cake and decorations were done, they'd go food shopping. Then they'd come home and frost the cake, wrap the presents and make dinner. All this had to get done before Meryl returned home.

Hours later, Mr. Vento was finishing up the final touches on dinner. Charlie was wrapping his mom's present and Gary was frosting the cake. Everything that needed to get done, got done. She would be home any moment.

Charlie came running in. "I heard the car; she's coming!"

Mr. Vento peeked out the kitchen window and watched the car roll up the driveway. "Here she comes!" he announced.

Gary just braced himself, waiting expectantly. He couldn't wait to see his wife's expression! The three guys stood together in front of the cake and yelled, "SURPRISE!" as she opened the door. Gary couldn't help but notice how beautiful his wife looked. She looked more relaxed than he'd seen her look in a long time, and she had make-up on her face and her nails were painted a cheerful pink. Her smile seemed to shine a little brighter, too.

"What is going on? What is this?" She stood there in shock, looking at the cake and at Mr. Vento in her apron. The great smells coming from the oven were delicious and all three men were beaming with pride.

"The three of us decided you deserved a special birthday, so why don't you go in to the living room and relax while I get you a glass of sparkling water with a lemon wedge, just like they do at the fancy salon. We all want to hear about your day at the spa," Gary motioned for her to head in to the living room. "We'll be there in a second." Then Charlie added with a giggle, "Make your self comfortable, Mom."

"Okay," she said, hoping they wouldn't be long. She was eager to tell them about her day.

A moment later, the three guys came in with birthday hats on their heads, serenading her with the "Happy Birthday" song. Gary gave her a birthday hat, which she wore proudly. Mr. Vento was sure to capture as much with his camera as possible. Charlie handed her the drink. Gary placed the presents before her.

She opened Dominic's present first. It was a large, rather heavy box. Underneath all the crumpled up newspaper pages, Meryl found individually wrapped pieces of china.

She unwrapped one piece and immediately recognized the white porcelain saucer adorned with red roses and a gold rim. Her smile widened as she unwrapped a tea cup with the same red rose pattern and gold rim. This was the same tea set Dominic used on the many occasions that the two of them sat together and shared a cup of tea.

"Dominic, I have admired this tea set of yours for years. Thank you very much!" she hugged Dominic.

"There are cake plates in there, too," he added. "My wife's father gave her the set a few years before he died. Louisa kept the tea cups out to keep the memory of her father near. She often used the cups for her afternoon tea. So I figured, I know how you enjoy your afternoon tea, and she would be so pleased to know you have them to use. It is a beautiful set." He smiled knowing he touched her heart.

"Mine's next, mine's next," Charlie excitedly handed his present to his mom. "You're gonna' love it, Mom!" He intently watched her open the gift.

"Hey, this is great! It's not often the three of us are in the same picture! Usually I'm the one taking the shot!" She smiled as she gazed at the photo of her family.

"Remember, that was after the Championship game. Mr. Vento took one of the three of us. That's a good one of me holding my trophy," Charlie boasted. His mom gave him a glare. "Oh," he added, "you and Dad look good, too!" He gave her an apologetic smile.

"It's a perfect one of all of us. Great idea. Thanks, Sweetie," she reached over to kiss Charlie on the cheek, "and thank you, Mr. Vento. Without you, we wouldn't have many photos around here."

"Dad's is next." Charlie gave his dad a coy smile and handed the small gift box to his mom.

Meryl carefully unwrapped the present and opened it to find a beautiful wedding band, similar to the one she lost years ago in the sandbox at the town playground.

"It's so beautiful. I miss wearing my wedding ring. But there always seemed to be more important things to buy." She placed the ring on her finger. "Look, it fits perfectly." It was hard for her to understand how Gary could have bought her a gift when they had been side by side every day, every hour, for months. "I don't know how or when you got this, but you're a pretty sneaky fella', Mr. Nelson!" Pointing to the other two she added, "And I think he received some help from his accomplices!" Everybody was laughing and accepting none of the blame!

Gary reached for her hand, "Wait a second, Honey; you didn't look inside the ring." He delicately removed the ring from her finger and read to her the inscription, "Surrender", then placed the ring back on her finger.

"I don't understand," Meryl said and gazed blankly at her husband.

Gary got up from the table, signaled to Charlie to play the Amy Grant CD that they'd already set up. Holding out his hand, he asked, "Dance with me?" The song *I Surrender All* played in the background.

She didn't answer, only followed his lead. Gary struggled with his balance on the make-shift dance floor, but to hold each other so closely was a gift both cherished.

Mr. Vento and Charlie gave them their privacy and went to the kitchen.

As they danced slowly and held each other tightly, Meryl asked, "Honey, what do you mean by "Surrender"?" Gary stared intently at her and explained, "I have to surrender all to God for the first time in my life. Listen to the words." As they swayed, he closed his eyes and sang to her.

He opened his eyes and admitted his deep feelings, "I surrender my situation, my future, my family, my doubts, my fears… everything. I always thought I was in control, but that was far from the truth. I must trust in His ways and know I am nothing without Him. I hope, one day, you too can surrender all to God, Meryl. It's not easy, I know, and I hope it doesn't take a situation such as mine to make you reach the same conclusion as I have."

She held him tightly and admitted, "I can't surrender. I don't want to surrender. To surrender will show I'm weak. I can't afford to be weak. I must be strong for you and Charlie. I'm afraid if I surrender, I may lose you. I can't lose you, Gary." She began to weep in his arms.

"Surrendering takes enormous strength because you're admitting you are weak and you realize that if you continue without surrendering to God, you will certainly lose. By surrendering to God, your weakness turns into strength. By surrendering, you are accepting the situation and handling the future as best as you can, while receiving blessings along the way. To surrender to God means you acknowledge He is in control, and you respect and honor His wishes for you." It took all of Gary's physical strength to continue dancing, and all of his emotional strength to continue this conversation with his wife.

"I don't know if I can," she confessed.

"I know; that's why I engraved the ring. It will be a daily reminder." He kissed the ring on her finger. The song ended and they remained embraced as the next song began. They were unaware of the bustling in the dining room. Eventually, everyone gathered at the dinner table where the birthday celebration continued, with all of Meryl's favorite foods on the menu.

As the end of the party drew near, Charlie's mom asked, "What's coming up in a few days, Charlie?" Charlie didn't know what she was hinting at. "The first day of ...," she waited expectantly for him to complete the sentence.

"School," he said, as he looked and sounded quite depressed.

"Oh, it's not that bad. You knew it was coming when we got your list of teachers in the mail last week. At least you know some kids in your classes. But listen, since it's pretty late now, why don't you head up to bed? I'll be up in a minute. Hopefully by the first day of school, we'll be back in to the routine of a decent bedtime during the week," she explained.

"You have got to be kidding me, Mom," Charlie protested. "Dad, talk to her! Mr. Vento, help me!"

"Sorry Charlie, she's right. Time for bed," his dad agreed. Charlie said good-night to everyone and headed upstairs.

"In fact, I'm going to bed myself because I am wiped." Walking over to his wife, he said, "Happy birthday, Honey. I hope it was a special day for you, because you're special to me."

She shined with happiness. "It was perfect!"

"Good night, Dominic. We had her fooled, didn't we?" Gary shook Dominic's hand.

"We sure did, Buddy. Good night." Dominic patted Gary on the back.

Gary turned around as he was leaving the kitchen. "Thanks for all of your help. I couldn't have done it without you."

"It was my pleasure. I had a great time," Dominic said as he continued to put leftovers in the refrigerator.

With only Meryl and himself in the kitchen, Dominic asked what was decided with Gary's job. Meryl explained how they agreed that he would take a leave of absence until he felt strong enough to return. Both wondered silently if that was even a possibility. When the room was back in order, Meryl thanked Dominic for the tea set and for helping her family make this a wonderful day. With a good-bye hug, she promised to call him tomorrow.

Meryl kissed Charlie good-night even though he was already asleep in his bed. Then she kissed Gary good-night only to find that he, too, was already asleep. She quietly lied in bed and reflected on her day. She fell asleep with a smile on her face.

Chapter Sixteen

"Charlie! Come on! You're going to be late AGAIN!" his mom shouted up the stairs. School had been in session for a month already, and nothing was routine yet, except dad being asleep when Charlie left. "If you don't leave soon, you'll be late!"

Charlie came running down the stairs. His mom stood there, holding his bagged lunch. He grabbed the lunch and jammed it into his backpack. She heard the crunch of chips and thought, *"So much for keeping the chips in tact."*

"Wait! I have to see Dad and say good-bye," Charlie said as he began to return upstairs.

"Just yell up to him; he's probably sleeping anyway. When you get home from school, you can talk with him." She was losing her patience.

"But…" Charlie knew he was really, really late this morning and didn't want to walk in after the late bell.

"BYE DAD!" he yelled up the stairs at the top of his voice. Charlie waited, but there was only silence. Frustrated, he grabbed his backpack and headed out the door.

Meryl yelled after him, "Love you! Have a good day." As she watched Charlie and the other neighborhood kids walk away, she thanked God for the beautiful day, the wonderful neighborhood, her husband, her son and Mr. Vento. Although she was going through a difficult time, she felt blessed.

Chapter Seventeen

Charlie could feel the sun's warmth on his face as he walked home from school. His backpack was exceptionally heavy today. It seemed as if all the teachers had the same idea: homework, and lots of it! He walked his usual route, down Mulberry Street, a right on to Oak, then a left on to Birch. Rounding the corner, he could see his house in the distance. As he got closer, he noticed Mr. Vento working in his front garden.

"Hi, Mr. Vento, what are you doing in the garden?" Charlie asked as he took a seat on the front porch steps.

"I'm getting the garden ready for winter. I finished raking this morning and am now planting some bulbs for next spring. How was school today?" Mr. Vento decided to join Charlie on the steps since he was in need of a break. He poured a glass of lemonade for each of them. As he leaned over to give Charlie his glass, Mr. Vento became aware that his back was already starting to ache.

Charlie thanked him for the drink and said, "It was all right. I have a ton of homework."

Sitting on the steps, Charlie admired the work Mr. Vento was doing to the garden. Charlie noticed that the fallen leaves and weeds no longer covered the garden floor. The bushes, which were recently very high and adorned with fragrant delicate flowers, and served as a visible treat to any one who passed by, were now cut to a short stubble. Charlie imagined how beautiful the garden would look in the spring when the newly planted bulbs would flower. He wanted to share the experience of creating beauty. That is when he came up with the idea, "Hey, Mr. Vento, can I help you plant?" Charlie asked.

"Sure. I can always use some help," Mr. Vento said as he slid the cold glass across his forehead. "My back is already starting to ache, and I still have to dig holes for a few rose bushes."

"Roses are Dad's favorite flower, red roses. He says they remind him of his mother, because she had a rose garden at his house when he was growing up. He told me it was a huge garden, and she would give bouquets to all the neighbors. There were red, pink, yellow, and I think white roses; all different kinds, too. We have one or two bushes in our backyard, but I'm sure it's nothing like what Grandma had."

Then he asked Mr. Vento excitedly, "Are you getting ready for another puppet show?"

"As a matter of fact I am. It is the first time I have been asked to perform for a church in town. They have a program that helps kids when they lose a relative or friend," Mr. Vento said as he took a sip of his drink. He continued, "The church is planning its schedule for next year and asked if I would do a puppet show in the spring. I agreed, but I need an idea for the show. I'm struggling because I want the kids to laugh and forget their heartache. Yet, I want to do a skit on death because I want them to know that they're going to be okay, that loved ones are near to support them, that there is hope. Losing someone is something every child who sees the show will have in common. I can't ignore that. Let me know if any ideas pop in to your head. Think about it, would you?"

In the midst of thinking of ideas for the show, Mr. Vento asked, "So how are your parents?"

"MY PARENTS!" Charlie exclaimed as he gulped down the remaining lemonade and jumped up from the stairs and headed for home. "I forgot I have to get home. They're probably wondering where I am! Sorry, Mr. Vento, I have to go. I'll be right back. I really want to help you with the garden, but I didn't get to see my dad this morning because he was sleeping."

"Okay, take your time." Mr. Vento said loudly. "Tell your parents I'm here if they need me." Charlie waved good-bye, and in a flash he was gone. Mr. Vento smiled and watched as Charlie's backpack bounced up and down on his back.

Charlie opened the front door and went inside. "Hey, Mom!" Charlie yelled, just like any other school day afternoon.

Charlie immediately became aware of an odd feeling in the house, one that he couldn't identify, almost a strange stillness. His mom didn't respond to his greeting; no one responded. Charlie didn't see anyone, hear anyone or smell any thing baking. This was odd… Where were mom and dad?

Walking further in to the house, he thought he may have heard crying. Who was crying? The uneasy feeling got stronger inside of Charlie. As he entered the kitchen, Charlie saw his mom sitting alone at the table. Her face was red, with tears streaming down her cheeks. She obviously didn't hear him coming.

"Mom, what happened? What's wrong?" There was fear and uncertainty in his voice.

Startled, Charlie's mom opened her eyes and stood to embrace her son. Then she just stood looking at him. As if he could read her mind, Charlie knew exactly what she was going to say. He looked deep within her eyes, and the fear turned to anger.

She said, "Charlie, I have something to tell you."

Immediately, he shouted, "Did he die?! Is my dad dead?!" He could feel the welling up of tears surfacing and his face getting bright red like his mom's.

"Charlie, he… he…" Her eyes filled with water.

"You didn't answer me. Is my dad dead?" He asked the question but wasn't sure if he wanted to hear the answer. Then his Mom said one word that would change his life forever.

"Yes," came softly from her mouth.

With hesitation she continued, "He's gone up to heaven."

Charlie had no questions, he had no statements. He just stared at her eyes, then realized her lips were moving. She was talking, but he only heard every other word, "sorry…, father…, bedroom…" Nothing was making sense. He shook his head from side to side.

"No, he can't be dead. I have to say good-bye. Why didn't you let me say good-bye this morning?" Charlie screamed through his tears.

Chapter Eighteen

As he was talking he heard his tone getting louder and meaner. "I wanted to say good-bye and you said, 'No, you'll have a chance to talk with him when you get home later on'," he said, mimicking his mother. "How could you do that to me? Why?!" He shouted at her as he stormed up the stairs to his bedroom. BANG! went his bedroom door, and Charlie threw himself on his bed, sobbing into his pillow. Mom always told him to punch his pillow when he was mad, so that's what he did now. Strength came from his arms like he never knew he had. Thump! Thump! Thump! With his eyes burning from the tears, he punched that pillow until he was breathing so heavily that he lost his breath. Exhausted, he collapsed on to his bed. The tears were just starting to slow down when there was a knock at his door.

"Charlie, can I come in?" Mom asked through the door in a gentle tone.

"No! Leave me alone!" He hollered in a voice that did not sound like his own.

As Charlie stared into his pillow and tasted the salt from his tears, he heard something slide under his door. All he wanted was to be left alone so he could lie on his bed and cry. But curiosity took hold, and he got up to see what it was. He picked up the envelope with "Charlie" written on it in his dad's handwriting. He quickly opened it and read, "Dear Charlie, I'm not feeling so strong these days, but today I decided to write you this letter while I still have some energy left in me. Usually I feel weaker, but today's not such a bad day. Son, I want you to know how proud I am of you. I was never one to tell you, and I don't want to miss another opportunity. You are a kind, young man who is honest and giving. With your brains and big heart, I have no doubt you will succeed in all you attempt to accomplish. I will be with you in spirit when you graduate middle school, high school and college. I will be with you when you marry the young woman of your dreams (yes, Charlie, there will be a day when you will fall in love), and on those bad days when life throws you a curve ball. On good or bad days, look up, Charlie, and pray! There is nothing in life that faith can not conquer. I will always treasure the memories we shared at the beach every summer, fishing on the lake, watching you play ball, and making huge ice cream sundaes on Friday nights. Be good to Mom. She will need your help around the house. Please try to be understanding, Charlie. She always does the best she can for all of us. Remember, you have lost a father, and she has lost a husband. You both are hurting right now and the two of you need each other. I love you, son, and will be watching from above. Dad." It was dated three months ago.

The tears started all over again, but this time he wanted his mom to hold him. Charlie opened his bedroom door and found his mother waiting expectantly for him to emerge. He ran in to her arms, and they both cried as they held each other tightly.

"He asked me to give that letter to you on the day he died. I don't know what it said, but it must be very special."

"It is." Charlie replied as he held it close to his heart.

They hugged each other until Charlie decided he wanted to be alone. His mom agreed, and left him in his room.

Moments later, Mr. Vento came over with a plate of brownies. He comforted Meryl as he joined her at the kitchen table. He saw she was busy talking with people on the phone, so he asked, "Would you mind if I saw Charlie?"

"Go right ahead. He might need you right now. He's in his room," she said as she pointed upstairs.

Chapter Nineteen

Knock, knock came the sounds from Charlie's bedroom door.

Mr. Vento waited until he heard a very sad, "Come in."

As Mr. Vento entered, Charlie sat himself up on his bed. "Hi, Charlie. May I join you?"

"Sure," Charlie mumbled as his eyes looked down.

Charlie was obviously a sports fan. His room was painted blue, with sports memorabilia covering his walls, shelves and desk. There were pictures of golfers, baseball and football players, autographed baseballs and boxes of baseball cards. Even his rug and lamp were in the shape of baseballs.

"I am so sorry to hear about your dad's passing. Your mom called me with the sad news after she spoke with you, when you got home from school. How are you doing?" Mr. Vento asked, as he sat down beside Charlie on the bed.

"I'm okay, I guess. I just don't get why I'm the only kid in my grade going through this..." As Charlie looked up, Mr. Vento could see his red, puffy, bloodshot eyes. "I just can't believe he died," Charlie continued. "I knew he wasn't feeling well; I could see he wasn't that strong and that mom and me had to help him with everything. I just always thought he would get better. Dads aren't supposed to die."

"I know it's a lot to accept, Charlie. Heck, even at my age, it's difficult to accept when people die. You're very young to be going through this, Charlie." Mr. Vento admitted. "Charlie, I never told you the story about how I became a puppeteer, did I?"

"No" Charlie said, not sure if he was truly interested in hearing the story right at this moment. But Mr. Vento thought it was an appropriate time for Charlie to know. "Years ago, I was a conductor of an orchestra. I loved classical music and lead a group of sixty musicians. They were so talented and played wonderfully together. Oh, it was beautiful... Anyway, among the violas, violins and cellos, there was one harpist. Her name was Louisa. Charlie, she was stunning. The first time I saw her, I didn't know which I fell in love with first: her beauty or the melody she made when she played that harp."

Charlie looked at Mr. Vento and noticed he was in a trance, looking like he was falling in love with Louisa all over again.

"We became great friends, and since we worked together, saw a lot of each other and would you believe, by the same time the following year we were married?" A smile came over Mr. Vento's face as he remembered how quickly he and his wife had fallen deeply in love. "We had such dreams, Charlie. We both wanted to have children, lots and lots of children. We wanted to open up a school of the arts for children to learn how to play, sing, act, and dance. Well, some of our dreams came true..., and some didn't. My wife died from an illness that came on suddenly. There was nothing the doctors could do for her, so I tried to make her as happy as I could for the days she had left. She died at home, just like your dad did. It was not an easy time for me or our kids, who were all around your age."

Charlie couldn't help but wonder what this had to do with Mr. Vento being a puppeteer, but he continued to listen.

"I still remember the night at the wake when my young niece sat on my lap and asked, "Why isn't Aunt Louisa moving?" My niece must have been three or four years old at the time. Well, I didn't know what to say to the little one. So I said, "Aunt Louisa was very sick. She died, but she's up in heaven now." And then Becky asked, "Can I go visit her in heaven today? I don't want her to be all alone." I said, "You can't visit her today, Honey; perhaps another day though. But don't worry, she's not alone. Aunt Louisa is with everyone who died that she ever loved. This makes her very happy in heaven." "So there are two Aunt Louisa's now!" Becky was jumping up and down. Aunt Louisa was one of her favorite aunts. "The one that doesn't move is here, and the one that does move is in heaven," Becky said, thinking she understood the concept of death. I tried explaining it to her by saying, "Her body does not move here on earth but when she died, God took the part of her that belongs to Him up to heaven." "Did you see God take that part, Uncle Dominic? When did He take it? Does she have a hole in her now?" Becky kept asking endless questions. I told her that no, I didn't see the Lord take this part of her, that it is something done in private with the person who died and Him. He took the part that belongs to Him, her soul, when she breathed her last breath. And no, there is no hole in her. The only hole is in our lives, the sadness that we feel, left by her absence. The soul is in heaven while the lifeless body remains here on earth."

Charlie watched as Mr. Vento pulled a handkerchief from his pants pocket and wiped his eyes. He had never heard someone explain what happens when a person dies.

"You still miss her, don't you?" Charlie asked the question, yet he already knew the answer.

"Every day, Charlie. Every day."

Charlie tried to imagine what Mr. Vento's wife was like. He had met their children only once, last year. They seemed pretty nice. Still trying to picture Louisa, Charlie asked, "How long has it been since your wife died?"

"Twenty years in March."

"And you're *still* crying?" Charlie didn't mean to sound rude; he just didn't understand and was surprised to see Mr. Vento's heartache after so many years.

"Yes, I'm still sad, but even though the feeling of loss doesn't go away, you are able to handle it a little better with each passing day. You have your good days and you're not-so-good days," Mr. Vento explained.

Chapter Twenty

"So, what does that story have to do with you becoming a puppeteer? Why didn't you continue to be a conductor?" Charlie was curious.

"Oh, right; I forgot my whole point..." Mr. Vento continued, "A few months after Louisa died, my heart was not in conducting or playing an instrument. I wanted to be left alone. But I had a dear friend, Robert, who wanted to perk me up, so he convinced me to start a hobby. When I was a boy, my father was a carpenter and showed me how to make furniture and toys. He would make different wooden puppets and marionettes for the neighborhood kids. I thought about this talent I always had but hadn't used in a very long time, and at Robert's insistence, I decided to make children's toys. Then, one of my customers suggested I put on puppet and marionette shows for the children. I didn't know how to do that. I was so scared, but I tried it and had a lot of fun. I got to see the children's happy faces and felt good about what I was doing. It has kept me busy ever since." At that moment, Mr. Vento had an idea, a really good idea. He was smiling. He was thinking about Becky, his talk with Becky, his puppets and the church puppet show.

Charlie saw Mr. Vento's expression change, like he just realized something. "What is it, Mr. Vento? What are you thinking?"

Mr. Vento replied, "I had a thought I'll share with you later, but in the mean time I wanted you to see that by me becoming a puppeteer, I am able to keep the memories of Louisa close to my heart and mind. I have a puppet named Louisa who plays the harp. And I know my wife would have enjoyed seeing all the children's happy faces at the puppet shows. I feel very close to her every time I perform. I tell you this because I know you will also figure out a way to keep your dad's memory alive."

Charlie gave Mr. Vento a hug, and they decided to head downstairs. Charlie helped himself to a brownie while Mr. Vento fixed two dinner plates, one for Meryl and one for Charlie. Then he went back home but not before giving a kiss good-bye to Charlie's mom and a great big hug to Charlie.

Aware of the empty seat, Charlie and his mom sat at the kitchen table and started to discuss plans for tomorrow. Charlie's mom mentioned that she was surprised someone from the funeral parlor hadn't arrived yet, and she wondered what was keeping them.

Charlie asked, "Why would they be coming to our house?"

Meryl told her son, "They are coming to pick up your father. He's still in the bedroom. They should have been here already."

Charlie was shocked. "Dad is in the house, and you didn't tell me?"

His mom explained, "I tried to tell you before, but you didn't hear me, Charlie. You were so upset."

Mom offered, "You can see him, Charlie, if you want. It would give you a chance to say good-bye. Would you like me to go with you to see him?"

Charlie, stunned, just nodded yes. He had never seen a real dead body before and was very scared.

Chapter Twenty-one

As Meryl opened the bedroom door, Charlie saw his dad lying on the bed. He was lifeless, and all Charlie could do was stare at his dad's still body. As they got closer to the bed, Charlie got closer to his mom. His dad looked so peaceful with his eyes closed. Charlie never noticed till then how thin his dad had gotten. He looked at his mom, who was sitting holding her husband's hand.

The phone rang and Meryl answered it. She decided to take the call downstairs, and left Charlie alone with his dad. Charlie wasn't as scared as he had been just a few minutes ago. There was something peaceful about seeing a resting body, Charlie realized, about seeing his dad in peace.

As he stared at his father's body, Charlie thought about Mr. Vento's explanation of death. How God took from Dad what belonged to Him, and now Dad's soul is with God in Heaven. Since there was no room on Dad's side of the bed, Charlie decided to sit on his mom's side. He sat for a long time, cross legged, just staring at his father's face and watching his still stomach. He smelled his father's Old Spice aftershave lotion. As his eyes slowly scanned the room, he noticed his father's wristwatch and favorite hard candies next to the phone; on the dresser, he saw his parent's wedding picture next to the family photo taken a year ago, and the family photo Charlie had given his mom for her birthday. In the closet he saw his dad's pants, shirts and old paint smocks. In the quiet stillness of the room, Charlie heard the commotion downstairs. The phone rang again; the door bell was buzzing; muffled voices came from below. He again got the letter that his dad had written and read it aloud as he recalled different memories they shared. Charlie started telling his dad about his day, just like he always did. He recited the poem he wrote in school about his dad, and about how Susie Jenkins threw up in the hallway as she ran to the nurse, and the good grade he got on the science test. He was able to tell his dad how much he loved him and missed him already. Charlie gave a little wave good-bye as he closed the bedroom door and headed downstairs.

Friends stopped by to see how the Nelsons were doing. Every one gathered in the kitchen to talk, cry and eat. There was a constant stream of people arriving and leaving. Everyone seemed sad but from the many hugs and dishes of food and offers to help, it was evident that Charlie and his mom were not going to go through this death alone. The loving community was coming together to support them and give them strength.

Chapter Twenty-two

The funeral parlor director came later that night to pick up Gary. It was hard to see him being taken away. Charlie was exhausted by the time his mom tucked him in, and she promised to keep him company in the still, quiet, dark room, till he fell asleep.

Staring at heaven through the darkness outside, he recalled, "When Mr. Vento came to my room, he talked about our soul. Do all souls go to heaven, Mom?"

"When we follow the Holy Spirit and live as God's children, our souls go to Heaven," she replied, but felt more of an explanation was necessary.

Unable to see her, Charlie could tell his mom was thinking. She was too silent. Then she said, "Charlie, God has given us many gifts, hasn't He?" In the darkness, Charlie nodded. "He's given us each other, this beautiful house, our health, our bodies and best of all, our lives. He's given us life, Charlie. He placed a beating heart in all of us. Without a beating heart, we would die. Well, God didn't stop there. He also gave each of His children the Holy Spirit which helps and guides us to live according to His will." Charlie's thoughts were racing. He still didn't quite understand. "Some of His children may not want to live as God wants us to live. He doesn't want to force His children to do something they don't want to. He has given us the freedom to make decisions for ourselves, using the Holy Spirit. We choose to follow it or not. Remember when you lied about Jimmy stealing your lunch money?" Charlie nodded yes again, even though his mom still couldn't see him. "He didn't steal it; you lost it, but chose not to tell the truth. Before you went to sleep that night, you told us the truth. The Holy Spirit was guiding you to do what was right, and you then chose to do what was right. The more we choose to listen and obey the Holy Spirit, the closer our soul is to God. We have a beating heart, the Holy Spirit, and a soul."

Charlie asked, "Before, when you said Dad was in heaven, did you mean his soul was in heaven?"

"Right. Daddy's heart stopped beating, so there was no more life in his body. Earthly life. But when he died, his soul went to heaven," Mom explained.

Charlie's questions continued, "Can we see the Holy Spirit or our soul?"

"No, we only see our bodies which contain the Holy Spirit and the soul. It's like our bodies are a vessel, a container that houses the soul."

"Then how do you know they're there? How do you know we have a Holy Spirit and soul?" It seemed the more answers Charlie received, the more questions he had.

Mom thought awhile, then asked, "Charlie, can you see the wind?"

Charlie looked out the window and saw the branches and leaves moving in the moonlight. "Sure, I can see the wind."

"Can you? You see branches and leaves moving. You hear wind chimes. When you're outside, you feel the wind against your face. You see its effects, you hear it, you feel it. But, if you think about it, you don't see the wind. You can't see wind because you can't see air. You're seeing the *effects* of the wind when you see branches sway and chimes chime. You can't see the wind, yet you know it's there by what it's changing. It's the same thing with the Holy Spirit and our soul. You can't see them, but based on how you live and the choices you make, it reveals if you are living according to how God wants you to live. That's the Holy Spirit and your soul."

Charlie was quiet for awhile. His mom started to get up, thinking he must have fallen asleep. But Charlie surprised her and said, "I guess you could say we are like puppets. God makes our bodies, like Mr. Vento makes the puppets. God gives us life, like Mr. Vento does by moving the puppets with his hands."

"That's true, Charlie. The only difference is that we get to choose what we do; the puppets have to follow Mr. Vento. They don't have a choice."

"Dad definitely lived how God wanted him to live," Charlie commented.

Charlie's mom smiled and agreed, as tears filled her eyes. She leaned over and kissed Charlie good night. "I love you, Charlie," she said.

"Love you too, Mom," Charlie said as she watched his eyes close.

Chapter Twenty-three

For the past two days, Charlie's routine was totally changed. At two o'clock in the afternoon, Charlie knew his class at school would be doing math. Well, not Charlie. He was at his dad's wake. He was greeted with the fragrance of flower arrangements displayed in the large room in front of the sea of chairs, rather than the familiar smell of elementary school and the rows and rows of desks. Some people were crying while others were talking. A low murmur was heard, like they were at the library. Charlie found this whole experience unsettling and didn't see the reason for such an affair. He didn't want to be here. He knew very few people and spoke to no one. There were one or two young children whom he didn't recognize anyway, who sat in the corner coloring. He stayed near his mom's side since that is where he felt the safest. Meryl stood near a big poster of photos of Gary's life, displaying Gary as a baby, at their wedding, and family snapshots where he was always smiling that big smile of his. Charlie decided to peruse the pictures.

As Charlie focused on this one funny picture of his dad riding a pony when he was a little boy, a hunched-over old man with crooked fingers patted him on the shoulder, shook his hand and said, "I'm sorry your father died. Now that you're the man of the house, take care of your momma."

Charlie didn't know what to say. He just stared at the man. *I'm* the man of the house? *I'm* taking care of Mom? *I'm* only 11! *I'm* not a man; *I'm* only a "young man." That's what Dad wrote. Emphasis on young! Panic struck from deep within.

Charlie's mom must have seen the dazed look on his face because she approached, with Mr. Vento behind her. "Charlie, Mr. Vento wanted to know if you'd like to go home with him now, and I'll come over and pick you up when I get home in an hour or so."

"Okay," he said, so grateful to get out of that place. He decided he would ask Mr. Vento at a later time what this man was talking about.

Chapter Twenty-four

Mr. Vento and Charlie took their coats off and sat in his living room. They decided to just relax and watch TV. The last thing Charlie remembered as he lied on the sofa was seeing a commercial for a really cool videogame.

Charlie awoke with a heavy, yet soft blanket over him and a fluffy pillow under his head. He heard rattling of dishes in the kitchen, smelled something really good, and noticed the sun had set. He wondered how long he had been asleep.

"Hi, Mr. Vento," he said as he entered the kitchen. Mr. Vento quickly turned around.

Watching Charlie shuffle in to the kitchen he said, "Hey, Charlie! Did I wake you?"

"No, the smell of what's cooking woke me. I'm starving!" Charlie took in a deep whiff of the kitchen aromas.

"Have a seat Charlie; the table is all set. Your mother should be over to join us any minute. I invited her so she could escape the commotion at your house." He set the table for three and, as if on cue, Meryl came to the door. Mr. Vento made a delicious meal, and it was the first time Charlie got to see his mom smile since his dad died. It was a wonderful dinner. They reminisced about good times shared with Dad. Some of the stories were funny, like last year when Gary was in the middle of building a shed from a kit and lost the directions with all the steps on how to build it. He asked Mr. Vento to come over and help put the many pieces of different size wood, nuts, bolts and hinges together to resemble the picture from the ad. It took the two of them all day to figure it out, and they still had a number of pieces left over! Meryl remembered watching them from the kitchen window. She said all they did for the first hour was scratch their heads!

Meryl was still chuckling when she got up and started clearing the dishes and cleaning the kitchen. Mr. Vento said, "Don't worry about this, Meryl. I'll take care of it."

Mr. Vento started to get up when Charlie asked, "Before you put everything away, can I have some more?"

Both of them were surprised that Charlie was still hungry and simultaneously said, "Of course you can!"

Mr. Vento added, "You need to eat, Charlie. A fine young man, such as you, needs his energy."

His mom grinned and said, "Dominic, would you mind if I head back to the house? This has been lovely, but I'm a bit tired."

Mr. Vento said, "That's fine. When he's done, I'll walk him over." She gave Mr. Vento a big hug and said, "Thank you for being such a great friend." Mr. Vento just smiled and replied, "You are quite welcome." After she left, Mr. Vento joined Charlie who was finishing his meal.

As he watched Charlie, he thought about how Gary won't see this young man grow in to a man. He won't be there to help Charlie learn to drive, or watch him graduate from high school or college. He will never meet Charlie's wife or children. So to himself, Mr. Vento prayed that God would place special people in Charlie's life, to walk him through these many milestones that he would face in the future. Mr. Vento was finished saying, "Amen" to himself when Charlie said, "Mr. Vento, can I ask you a question?"

"Sure Charlie," he said, still focused on his previous thoughts.

Charlie asked, "What does it mean to be 'the man of the house'?"

Confused, Mr. Vento asked, "Where did that come from? I said a 'fine young man' not 'the man of the house'. Did that puzzle you?"

"At the wake, a man told me I am now 'the man of the house' and to take care of mom. I don't know what to do or even how. Do I have to quit school? Do I have to go out and work, like my dad did? I can't even drive yet! I don't even know how to tie my own tie." Charlie started talking faster and a look of fright came upon his face.

"Charlie," Mr. Vento said as he placed a hand on his shoulder, "you won't have to quit school or go out and work. What the man meant to say was that you are mom's big helper now. You'll be a man some day, some day very soon, you're just not a man right now. You're a young man and you can help your mom as a young man can. For instance, instead of just sitting at the table waiting for her to bring your dinner, you can set the table, or put the dirty dishes in the dishwasher without being asked, or make your bed without being reminded, or be on-time for school or help tend the garden. Every day, try to do a few things like that to help your mom. That's what the man was telling you. You'll be a man some day, some day very soon; you're just not a man right now."

Charlie thought about this for a moment. Mr. Vento heard him release a sigh of relief.

Sensing the panic gone, Mr. Vento asked with a smile, "So, can I offer you something else?"

"No, I'm stuffed! That was really good," Charlie said as he patted his tummy. "I should be getting home to mom."

"All right. Let's get you home." Mr. Vento grabbed his sweater as Charlie opened the door and felt the cool fall air on his face.

Charlie yelled, "Good-bye!" and waved to Mr. Vento. As he entered the house, Charlie became aware of how his house was transformed. When he entered the kitchen, the aroma of food was overwhelming: fruit baskets, cookies, cakes, and pasta dishes. The many bouquets of flowers throughout the house added beauty, different scents, and life to a house filled with grief and sadness.

"That was a nice night, wasn't it?" his mom asked, as he joined her on the couch.

"It was just what I needed," he replied. The two of them sat together and then quickly became aware of how tired they were.

"Okay Charlie, it's very late and time for bed. Up you go."

Charlie did a half-hearted protest and then, thinking about his recent discussion with Mr. Vento, proceeded to head upstairs. Charlie wanted to make sure he helped his mom instead of making it harder for her.

His mom joined him in his room a few moments later. Sitting on the edge of the bed, his mom asked, "You okay, Charlie?"

Answering honestly, he told her, "Yeah, I'm good. I just really miss dad, but having everyone around helps me. It's when I'm alone that it bothers me the most."

"I don't like the night time or being alone either, Charlie. It was always difficult for me, on the few occasions, when your dad and I slept apart." Mom acknowledged, "I miss your dad sleeping beside me. The bed seems so big right now."

After giving it some thought, Charlie suggested, "Would you want to have a sleepover in my room tonight? You can sleep in the bed, and I'll set up the sleeping bag on the floor." Mom loved the idea! They set up his room and settled in for the night.

Chapter Twenty-five

The next few days seemed to drag on and on for Charlie. Many people attended the funeral and the gathering at their house. There were more strange faces, like the man at the wake, who knew Charlie but Charlie didn't know them. Every day, Charlie expected his dad to come through the front door yelling, "I'm back everyone! Surprise!" But it never happened.

Meryl wrote many "thank you" cards to those who baked a meal, sent flowers, helped with the funeral arrangements and the reception, delivered groceries and helped clean the house. While seeing the stack of stamped cards become higher and higher, she realized how fortunate she and Charlie were to be surrounded by such wonderful and caring people.

Meryl waited until he missed his friends and felt more like himself to send Charlie back to school. On his first day back, every one hugged him and offered words of sorrow. His classmates gave him a giant home-made sympathy card. Charlie really appreciated it. He felt sad in school but enjoyed having his routine back. Being with his friends helped ease the pain of missing his dad.

Days turned into weeks. Weeks turned into months. As time passed, the grief did not go away. It seemed to always linger, just like Mr. Vento said it would. Charlie tried to get used to the emptiness in his life. He continued to live and enjoy life because he knew his dad would want him and his mom to be happy. But some days, Charlie still felt sad inside.

Charlie was passing Mr. Vento's house on his way home from school one day when he heard the screen door open and a loud, "Charlie!" behind him. Mr. Vento came barging on to the porch yelling, "Come, I have to show you something in my garden." They walked past an assortment of bushes and flowers of all different shapes, colors and sizes.

Before Charlie could get a word out, Mr. Vento was standing next to a beautiful red rose bush on the side of his house. Its blooms were many, with a delicate fragrance, yet strong enough to be smelled from a distance.

"Wow, Mr. Vento. That is amazing! I don't think I've seen so many roses on one bush before! Our bushes at my house sure don't look like this! And the flowers are huge!" As he placed his nose near its center, Charlie gently touched the many velvety soft petals of one rose.

Mr. Vento explained, "The last time you saw this bush was the day your dad died, Charlie. I was planting it in my garden. Remember?"

Charlie tried to recall, but it had been many months since then. After some thought, he exclaimed, "I do remember! I was supposed to help you plant it, but I never did."

"Well, that day I planted it in his memory. Isn't it gorgeous? I wonder if this is what one of the bushes looked like at your Grandma's house." Mr. Vento stood back, admiring the beautiful bush.

"Let me make a big bouquet for you and your mom. You can explain to her where it came from." Mr. Vento got his clippers and created a heaping pile of roses.

As he was doing this, he shared with Charlie, "Do you remember, a while ago, I told you about the puppet show at the church for kids who've lost a loved one?" Not looking at Charlie or waiting for a response, he continued, "Well, it's next week."

Charlie asked, "You haven't done that show yet? I thought that was months ago."

"That was when they asked me to do it. Now it's time for the performance," Mr. Vento explained. "Did you know that you helped me create a story for the show?"

"I did? What story? I didn't tell you any story. You sure it was me?" Charlie thought Mr. Vento was mistaken.

"Oh, I'm sure, Charlie. It was the night your dad died. You and I were in your bedroom, talking about the conversation I had with my niece, Becky, at my wife's wake. Becky had questions about her Aunt Louisa's death, and I answered them. I realized as I was talking with you, that it made a great story to help explain what happens to God's children when we die. We resemble a puppet and at death, it's like the puppeteer removes the hand from the puppet. It is then that our souls unite with God." Mr. Vento seemed to recall the memory well.

Charlie interjected, reciting his Mom's words, "But a puppeteer controls the puppet; God does not control His children."

Mr. Vento smiled and said, "That's right. God allows us to choose right from wrong. We'll work that important message in to the show. I hope this gives the children hope and an understanding that life doesn't end when our bodies die. Life continues in heaven when our soul is with God for eternity. If your loved one is with God, you know they are in good hands. I also want the children to know that their life here will be okay, since there are many people all around that will continue to care for them and love them." Mr. Vento cut the last of the roses and handed the bunch to Charlie, who needed both hands to support the bouquet.

Chapter Twenty-six

He pushed his elbow in to the doorbell. A few seconds later the door opened.

"Delivery!" came a familiar voice hiding behind the beautiful flowers, "For the best mom in the world."

"Oh, my heavens!" Charlie's mom said. "Where did these come from? They're gorgeous."

As Meryl arranged the flowers in a vase, Charlie explained the story of Dad's rose bush in Mr. Vento's garden. Charlie gave his mom a kiss on the cheek, "You like them?" he asked.

"I love them, and I love you, too!" she said and gave him a great big hug and kiss.

As Charlie ran off to watch afternoon TV, Meryl noticed how the sunlight fell upon the roses, enhancing their beauty. A sparkle caught her attention. It was her wedding ring, glistening in the sunlight. She removed the ring from her finger, and recalled her birthday celebration when Gary explained the significance of the word "surrender". How peaceful her husband looked when he conveyed his concerns, and surrendered to the faulty idea that he was in control. The trust Gary had in God brought more than peace; it also brought hope to Gary's heart. Meryl remembered how fearful she was to surrender her situation to God. Admiring her ring, she smiled and realized she was now ready, ready to surrender all. Although her heart ached and she missed her husband, seeing the roses inspired her to trust that their future would be filled with abundant blessings, just like the rose bush.

Charlie returned to the kitchen for a snack. While crunching on a carrot, he asked his mom, "Can we make a rose garden in the backyard? For dad, you know?"

As both took a moment to gaze at the bouquet of hope, Meryl smiled, kissed her ring and said, "That's a great idea, Son."

Printed in the United States
143107LV00001B/2/P